HERE ME

SHAKIL

Copyright © Shakil
All Rights Reserved.

This book has been published with all efforts taken to make the material error-free after the consent of the author. However, the author and the publisher do not assume and hereby disclaim any liability to any party for any loss, damage, or disruption caused by errors or omissions, whether such errors or omissions result from negligence, accident, or any other cause.

While every effort has been made to avoid any mistake or omission, this publication is being sold on the condition and understanding that neither the author nor the publishers or printers would be liable in any manner to any person by reason of any mistake or omission in this publication or for any action taken or omitted to be taken or advice rendered or accepted on the basis of this work. For any defect in printing or binding the publishers will be liable only to replace the defective copy by another copy of this work then available.

Thanks to Almighty God

Contents

Foreword

I like to take each and every platform to give something new to the audience, this is one among them.

Preface

A love story you would have never read before!

CHAPTER ONE

HERE ME

Here me, I was there during the tragic incident happened. "Sheeba" her name, my everything but.... and still. She came to China for an onsite work as she was working in an IT – company. There she met Muskhan for the first time, yes it was I! and China was my native, "LOVE AT FIRST SIGHT" was exactly the thing happened there. She had her first glance and got attracted towards me. 'Hi' she said. Actually, I had not received her "hi" as I was listening to the bird's chirping sound. It wasn't intentional as nobody had said "hi" to me before and so I didn't pay attention towards her.

Tak

Dok

Tuk

Exactly this was what I heard, a haiku from her heels.

Poetic Scene it was, a melodrama kind of. A mesmerizing bamboo flute music in the background was played by someone. I could feel the air entering the flute from one end and turning out into a music on the other end, What a process!

I didn't know whether it was been played from earlier and I listened to that then or she played it to match the scene.

But it had a sync.

She came near to me and that's it, rest was fast, we had travelled together from China to Mumbai, her place. As an orphan these days it was very special to have someone who actually cared you. "The first showers of the rain in the worst futile land" that was how I felt. In spite of my disability, she loved me I knew it was quite dramatic but it was true. I thought my blindness didn't bother her. She lived in an apartment in Mumbai and her door number was D seventy-three and I wasn't sure whether it was 703 or 73 or 373. She said this number once to someone for a delivery. She stayed alone in the house BC (Before China) and AC (After China) I joined her. She actually gave a good space in her house and I enjoyed it too.

H

Then slowly I started to adapt her routine, she wished me "Good morning Mushkan" every day and she would spend some time with me before and after office. After returning from office, she would start doing some work in her laptop and throughout the night I heard the keys sound from the keyboard. She cared me a lot and I could feel the motherliness at the times she was near me. Whenever I was feeling low, she came and showered her love towards me. I had always felt that I had a person right behind me every time and for everything. We discussed a lot of things; she would share her happy moments and sad moments to me as well. At first, I found difficult to understand her language but as the days went, I understood it. She always showed me the best of her smile, best of her care, best of her words. She was the light in my life. She was the only one who touched me and played with me Usually, I would be treated as untouchable, no one would touch, talk and even hear me. She was the one who respected and responded me.

Whenever I spoke my curse mode was activated; leading to confusions whether I was dumb or the people around me were deaf as they won't respond me but she came in my life and changed out everything. I always wanted to ask about her parents but I feared her separation as she would get remined and moved towards them. How selfish I was but I didn't want to lose her.

Separation after togetherness was like death after life to me. She was like honey to the hunger and money to the beggar. I knew I became more poetic after listening to the poems she used to read aloud. She was a big fan of Bharathiyar's poems, she made many of his poems into songs that fit into her own tune and she used to hum it all-day.

Everything was fine until the day arrived. The day which made me an orphan again.

As per her daily routine, she returned home from office.

'Bye. Let's talk tomorrow! I have lots of work tonight.'

She took her laptop and started doing her work. The sound of the key made me possessive; she was spending time with a non-living thing more than spending time with me. In between the keys sound I heard a thud.

Ding dong.

I realized that someone was waiting outside the door. She stood from the chair, I assumed to be as I heard a scrape.

Ding dong.

She went towards the door, as soon as she opened it, I heard a sound but this time a scream. Yes, it was from my girl Sheeba. 'What happened' I shouted but there was no reply from her. This was the first time a she didn't reply to me. I wanted to know the situation there. So, I started to observe the sounds carefully. Sheeba was pushed down by someone and the door was locked. She shouted 'Help Help ...'. The one who entered our house replied 'SSSHHHH'. 'We gave you many chances but you refused.' It was a male voice.

'Aadhitiyan, Please leave me'

'Think of the things you did to us, you created a bad opinion about our industry, you provoked an investigation, you collected the evidence against us and you made people to file complain against our industry.'

'I just wrote the truth; many innocent people have been affected due to your industry and —'

'Hmm, you did your work, Lemme do mine as well'

I noticed a piece of silence there, the most horrible silence it was.

The clock's tick-tock made the loudest noise there and each tick synced with the heartbeat.

'Don't kill me please' Sheeba started to scream again.

I guess he might had taken a weapon and he was marching towards Sheeba.

"Tak"

"Dok"

"Tuk"

The same but this time with more bass and melancholy kind of. Each step splashed vengeance and anger. When he was advancing each step, I prayed 'God this couldn't happen to her'. On the four step I was facing him directly but he didn't mind. He crossed me and moved. I heard rumbling sounds of lot of things falling on the floor with addition to Sheeba's scream. I can't do anything to save her as my legs were tied. 'Leave her! If you are dare enough then untie my legs' but again my curse started to work there as he can't hear me.

'I beg you! please don't kill me, I will delete all the feeds in my ....' she said.

Quickly something splashed on my face, yes, it was her blood and Sheeba felt down. The shoes hurried towards the door and the killer escaped from the scene. All I did throughout this massacre was to scream and beg him to leave her. I felt ashamed of my inability to save her. The force on which her blood hit shaked me and my last ray of hope got literally killed.

After long time police had arrived our house, they checked her laptop and they discussed that Sheeba was running a blog and in that she spoke up for the people. She read Bharathi poems as a motivation or Bharathi poems made her to fight against injustice? I was thinking that. She was my kannamma.

I could still feel the touches we had together, her smile and her voice. Earlier I was an orphan she cared for me, she loved me but now after her loss of physical appearance, I became how actually I was.

Her profession made us united but her passion made us separated. She was my everything still and forever.... Police were searching for the culprit, I was shouting 'It was Aadhitiyan' but they too can't hear me. It was my curse that no one could listen and even consider me. Everyone treated me as invisible but actually I was not.

The only person who listened and replied me was she, Sheeba. Only she could listen me and I would be waiting for her forever by just saying to all 'HEAR ME'.

Avoid confusions, I am Pilea Peperomioides, just Google me!

I did this short story just to remind that humans are one among the living things, not only the living thing!

Even if it may be a plant, tree, animal, bird, or what ever it is, they too have their own life, Respect it.

Don't expect every living thing to speak or express its feelings.

and YES,

My Final Note :

The world is not only for humans

Bye, Until my next work strikes you.

Thank You!

www.ingramcontent.com/pod-product-compliance
Lightning Source LLC
Chambersburg PA
CBHW020949160726

47993CB00007B/3004